bitch.

an inner voice fantasy

by Cecelia Hendryx

Woman's Work Productions

BITCH. AN INNER VOICE FANTASY
By Cecelia Hendryx

PUBLISHED BY: WOMAN'S WORK PRODUCTIONS
Contact: C J PRODUCTIONS
25600 Woodward Avenue, Suite 101
Royal Oak, Michigan 48067
248/258-2494

TO ORDER BOOKS OR BITCH MERCHANDISE: Call toll-free, **1-888-32-BOOKS**
See last page for *BITCH* **merchandise selections**

Copyright 1995 by Cecelia Henderson
First Printing 1995   Second Printing 1997   Third Printing 1998
Printed in the United States of America
Library of Congress Cataloging-in-Publishing Data
Hendryx, Cecelia
Bitch. An inner voice fantasy / by Cecelia Hendryx--1st edition

ISBN 0-9648527-7-2 $12.95

1. Humor   2. Political Commentary   3. Social Commentary   4. Women

When I get into discussions with men,
I always hold my position, and they usually
end up saying something *outrageous* like:
"Oh, you think your life, your concerns, your dreams
and your opinions are more important just because
you're a woman!"
After I calm them down, I can explain to them,
"Yes."

If you can't have things
your way,
why have them at all?

Low self-esteem can be a major
problem for a woman.
You could be as rich, talented and
beautiful as somebody like Whitney Houston.
But if you have low self-esteem,
you could end up marrying somebody like...
like... Bobby Brown.

Jane Fonda is an accomplished woman
in her own right.
And when people ask her how she landed
multi-Billionaire Ted Turner, she should
not hesitate to tell them
that it was probably because
she did it the old-fashioned way —
she sucked dick.

Men say all women want from them is money.
I used to dispute that.
But then I thought, "Well..."

You might as well marry a rich man.
Any man is still only a man.
He might as well have money.

Women overlook their most powerful weapon
with men.
Pussy.
They want it.
We've got it.
It's supply and demand.
And we've been demanding too little
for what we supply.

Romance?
Men are only as romantic
as they need to be
to get the pussy they want.

There was a time when men romanced women
by bringing them flowers and
arranging candlelight dinners.
But now, a romantic date is when
the whole evening passes, and the guy hasn't tried
to force your mouth to his crotch.

I, too, am looking for
a few good men.
But I will settle for
finding just one.

A recent article advised women to avoid
potentially abusive relationships by selecting
men who aren't jealous, controlling,
violent, or users of sexist language.
Great.
But what would be their advice
before that new crop of men gets in from Saturn?

John Wayne Babbitt claimed his wife Lorena chopped
off his penis because she didn't come during sex that night.
But if women sliced off penises
whenever men failed to sexually satisfy them,
every man would be pissing through a straw.

Things men do that women never would:
Do drugs and party with the money donated for
co-joined twin daughter's separation surgery;
smash golf clubs through
another motorist's windshield (Jack Nicholson);
kill and eat people (Jeffrey Dahmer); bomb and kill
babies in the Middle East (George Bush); watch sports
on TV from September to September (every man).
Things *women* do that men never would:
Give birth.
Put up with men.

Behind every great man is
a greater woman who was held back.

There are two true types of conservatives.
Either they are white men miserable with themselves,
who want to make sure
everybody else is miserable too,
or... Well, maybe there's only one type.

Rush Limbaugh --
The disgustingly fat,
racist, sexist white man's
last best hope.

Howard Stern --
the scrawny, pinch-faced,
racist, sexist white man's
last best hope.

Abortion. Woman must keep the right to choose.
But the most important choosing should
take place before pregnancy.
Woman share their bodies with such losers.
We should have minimum standards, or something.
Of course, if women had any standards,
most men wouldn't be able to get laid.

There are progressive men who support
a woman's right to choose abortion.
Take Bill Clinton, for instance.
Of course, when you have as many
women-on-the-side as he does, you'd
want to keep this kind of option open.

Bill Clinton is probably the one President who
could admit to his extramarital affairs
and get away with it:
"Okay, I did sleep with those other women --
but I didn't come!"

The half-brother and half-sister of Bill Clinton's
who've popped up should make his relationship
with daughter Chelsea closer.
Because he'll be able to relate to
how she's gonna feel when her
half-brothers and half-sisters start popping up.

Feminist Betty Friedan's ex-husband
expressed great disappointment in her as a wife
by saying that in their entire 20-year marriage,
she hadn't cooked 10 meals or washed 10 dishes.
I'm disappointed in her, too. Why hasn't she
shown other women how to accomplish that?

Feminists want the world to be woman-centered.
But how come, when feminist Barbara Streisand
made her movie, "The Prince of Tides,"
it was about a man?

And women have praised that movie "The Piano"
because it was written by, directed by
and starred women.
But a story about a woman who *chooses*
to remain silent?
Now, that's a men's movie if I ever heard of one.

A woman in a position of power
is of no use,
if she might as well be a man.

If every woman in America went to see
"The Last Seduction,"
Gloria Steinem would be
out of a job.

Someone asked who is the type of man
for the 90's: Arnold Schwarzenegger,
Jerry Seinfeld or Woody Allen?
Well, at least Jerry Seinfeld's teenage girlfriend
is not his daughter, like Woody Allen's.
And Arnold -- forget it.
The only part of him he *can't* pump up happens to be
the only part women are really interested in.

So Woody Allen excuses having sex with
his daughter by saying:
"The heart wants what the heart wants."
Somehow, Woody got
his body parts confused.

Like Jerry Seinfeld, men are pursuing younger and younger girls these days. And it's a smart move on men's part. How else are they going to find females whose minds haven't been screwed over by them already?

Women actually prefer younger men.
Men think that's because a younger man
can "keep it up" all night.
But really, given a choice,
women like men who aren't losing their hair.

One advantage to marrying younger men
is that they will already know how
you're going to look when you're older.
Of course, there's still the problem of what they
are going to look like.

A survey found that 80% of women
would prefer anything over having sex.
But that's not because women can't enjoy sex.
It just means they don't enjoy it with
the insensitive, pot bellied, beer-burping, cheap, or
balding guys that 80% of women
do have sex with.

After seeing "Indecent Proposal,"
many women said they wouldn't sleep
with Robert Redford for a million dollars.
These are the same women who are having
sex with their beer-bellied, plumber-husbands,
hoping to get a new refrigerator or a tune-up
on their 10-year old station wagon out of it.

A woman's position in life is inevitably tied
to whichever man she sleeps with.
You have sex with a plumber, you get to
have the toilet fixed free-of-charge.
You give head to a big-time Hollywood producer,
you get to be called co-producer of
"Driving Miss Daisy," and win an Oscar.

There's so much criticism of a woman who
sleeps her way to the top.
But, in this society, what's the other way?

I feel sorry for lesbians who want to sleep
their way to the top, because
there are so few women at the top.
Of course, Madonna's at the top, but since she's
trying to have sex with every man *and* woman in
America, the wait is twice as long.

Professor Camille Paglia says Madonna
is the best leader for women because,
"Madonna knows how to get what she wants."
So, if, for example, women want equal pay
and decent child care, then we should
just shake tits and ass, and sleep with
every man we meet?
Oh, is that all!

Madonna tried to get her ex-husband, Sean Penn, back.
Our role model, Madonna, showing us that you
should be big enough to beg a man to
take you back -- and just overlook that
he might have trussed you up like a turkey
and beat the hell out of you.

Lorena Bobbitt was found not guilty
by reason of temporary insanity when she
sliced off her husband's penis after he beat and raped her.
And she had to have been temporarily insane --
she didn't kill him.

Many men have expressed fear
that women might cut them
like Lorena Bobbitt did her husband.
Why?
Those men aren't beating and raping women,
are they?

With Lorena Bobbitt's acquittal, the woman who says
William Kennedy Smith raped her
probably wishes she had broken that vase she
grabbed at the Kennedy compound.

Men who are first-time batterers
would never do it a second time if
my preventative proposal were instituted.
It's called the "Bullet-in-the-Brain" program.
It's an alternative to the
old "Slice-off-his Penis" program,
which John Wayne Bobbitt has shown
is not a deterrent.

Nothing succeeds like revenge.

They have Barbie dolls with dresses, high heels
and makeup to teach girls how to
be pretty and dainty. And the GI Joe dolls
come with guns and knives to teach boys
how to be tough and destructive.
But actually, the Barbie dolls should come equipped
with the stuff the GI Joe dolls come with--
so that girls can be prepared to deal with the
real-life GI Joe types they're going to
have to date, marry, work for...

Men treat women as if they're all alike
because, no matter her individual talents or desires,
a woman is going to have to do things their way.
While women treat men as if
they're all alike, because...
they are.

Why do women listen to men?
Like when a man tells a woman she's getting
too big for her clothes, she goes on a diet
and loses weight.
But when was the last time a woman told a man
he's getting too thin on top, and
he went out and grew hair?

Women will do anything to lose weight and attract men.
They consume all those diet foods and drinks.
risking cancer from those carcinogens in diet products.
But what's a little cancer?
It eats up a lot of fat.
Of course, it eats up every other part of your body, too,
but at least you will be thin.

When I explain to men that
the reason those really, really thin women can go on
to model become movie stars, or end up with rich men
is that they use this technique
where they don't swallow,
men will insist, "Of course, they swallow."
But I'm talking about food.

Men don't respect women because
women aren't assertive enough.
There's only one way
a man will respect a woman:
if she *demands* it --
right after she gets up off her knees
and rinses out her mouth.

Now there are TV ads for yeast infection creams.
But if women didn't have sex with men -- who,
let's fact it, will fuck anything that moves --
or doesn't -- women wouldn't get those diseases.
"Yeast infection" is just a code created by doctors
which really means, "So you've been letting
that filthy scum do it to you again!"

Women should just stop cooperating.
Don't work for unequal pay; refuse to do housework
if men won't share it; don't anticipate a man's
every whim; and, most importantly, deny men sex.
Of course, most women would then be unemployed,
battered, without homes or children --
or worse, in the street with their children.
But, what the hell, we'd be right...

I'll never understand men.
On the one hand, with all the progress
made in the women's movement, with better
educations and the inroads made by females into
the political and business worlds --
Why are men still only
interested in women for sex?
On the other hand, I'll never understand women,
either. Why aren't we all lesbians?

A man is like a dress
you buy at a crowded department store sale.
In your rush, you might think you got a really good deal --
until you get him home...
and try him on.

I could learn to tolerate men better, if only
they would learn their place —
and stay in it...
until *I* tell them to stop.

It's just like that old saying:
Men. You can't live with them...
You can't experience sexual dissatisfaction
without them.

Prostitution could be a panacea for women,
if handled the right way.
Instead of dating or marrying one insensitive clod
and putting up with him for 24 hours a day, year
after year, you could get paid good money,
and not have to deal with any particular man
for more than 5 minutes at a time.

Why do women date men they meet in singles bars?
It never leads to the altar.
Guys could tell you,
any man who frequents single bars
is *already* married.

In marriage, a woman is required to do
all kinds of things for her husband —
like have sex with him every
couple of months.

Never have a baby with a man unless
he is the kind of guy
you want to be involved in your life —
even years later,
when you hate his guts.

In a divorce, a husband can easily
scare his wife
if he demands
custody of their children.
But the wife
can only scare her husband
if she agrees to it.

Speaking of divorce,
a good woman's film on the subject
is "Intersection," because
the ending is so rewarding. On his way
to rendezvous with the Other Woman,
the husband gets killed
in an excruciatingly painful car crash.
Now, that's the way to end a marriage!

Man-bashing.
It's a dirty job.
But somebody's gotta do it.

Women are too timid. When they come up
against the glass ceiling,
they should remember
that a hammer beats the hell out of glass every time.

Sometimes women
should be more like men, especially white men,
who have bravado to spare.
Of course, if women had a system grounded in
the exploitation and oppression of the rest of the
world for the last 800 years backing them up,
they'd be pretty confident, too. Goddamn it!

But how can we expect the system to make way for
all the competent women out here?
What would we do with all these marginal
white men who have so many of the good jobs?
The whole damn society would be changed —
shaken to its very foundation. And,
of course, we can't have that —
that would be the way it should be.
Too un-American.

Women always gripe about wanting to do
everything men do. But sometimes, we should
be glad we aren't able to do some things men do.
Take the Catholic priesthood. We would have to
lie about molesting altar boys.
And then there's golf.
We'd have to pretend to enjoy knocking
a little ball around with a stick for hours,
and wear ugly clothes while doing it.

Some things women want to be left out of by men.
Like having to see who can drink the most
six-packs during Monday Night Football, and then
counting how many times we belch or take a piss.
And we'd have to have hairy asses and fat bellies
to scratch afterwards, too. If we lived in the
South, we'd have to ride in a rusted-out pick-up truck,
have rotted teeth, and yell obscenities out the
window, scaring the hell out of unsuspecting
people on the street.

What is this whole women-in-the-military and
women-as-fighter-pilots thing?
Or for that matter, the gays-in-the-military thing?
Oh, yeah. "We want the right to kill
Third World people for the benefit of greedy
multinational corporations and selfish, over-consuming
Americans, too!"

Gay men. Now that's a quandary.
How can one man stand himself,
much less an extra one?

About that man in the Midwest trailer park
whose two children killed him after
years of his abuse --
In court, lawyers debated just how many
beatings and stabbings would justify
those kids shooting their dad. But really, now,
any man who would force his kids
to live in a trailer park
deserves whatever he gets.

Several Midwestern states require that a teenage girl
get the permission of her parents
if she needs to get an abortion.
I can see it now,
a 14-year old in the Bible Belt asking her father:
"Daddy, can I abort your baby?"

Dr. Kevorkian -- arrested for assisting suicides in Michigan. But it's no wonder the authorities want to prevent him from doing business.

Michigan is in the Midwest.

It's dark, it's cold, it's provincial, and it's BORING. If they didn't have a law against assisted suicides, hordes of Michigan citizens might beg to be put out of their misery, and there wouldn't be any taxpayers left.

The movie industry, television writers and food
companies use the Midwest
as their American standard.
Why?
People who live in the Midwest don't even
like their pointless lifestyle. They wish
somebody would do something to change it,
not accommodate it.

Nobody asked Toto if he wanted to
go back to Kansas.

Journalists take themselves so seriously.
Why? We don't.
Especially the so-called broadcast journalists.
Take the furor over Connie Chung doing the news
with Dan Rather. What?!
How many credentials do you need
to read a TelePrompTer?
What do Dan Rather, Tom Brokaw and Peter Jennings
have that Connie doesn't? Oh... yeah...

Speaking of the male-dominated media.
When Lorena Bobbitt was acquitted for chopping off
her husband's penis -- they certainly didn't break into
the broadcasts to announce it.

A recent news story reported on
yet another priest who
molested boys in his parish.
By now, it's only news when
a priest is found who's
not molesting boys in his parish.

American teenagers today have no spunk,
no courage, no sense of rebelliousness.
How can they stand by without protesting
this proliferation of TV talk shows?

Though men say all women do is talk,
no women were considered as host
of any of those treasured late night talk shows.
Of course, to host a talk show, you do have to let
somebody else get a word in edgewise.

A guest on a talk show said she teaches
how to steal men from other women.
But how does she make a living?
Can't be much of a commission
on petty theft.

Some think I shouldn't say such things
about men. Oh. Men can kill thousands in wars;
addict teenagers to drugs, alcohol and tobacco;
shoot people over "manhood" issues;
and watch televised sports
from September to September;
but they can't take a joke.

Could I say some jokes on women now?
Sure--men!

In answer to the women's movement,
there's a men's movement, where a lot of white
men meet and learn to "bond" better.
As if the way they've raped and exploited the entire
world together over the last 800 years was
just not done well enough.

David Letterman jokes about how he got
speeding tickets in Connecticut.
But he's lucky he was not in L.A.
He might still be recovering from deadly
police baton headblows.
But, then again, *he* is a *white* guy.

And Jane Fonda claims that Ted Turner
is the man of her dreams. She can't be looking
at the same, wrinkled up guy we are.
Has to be that she looked at
the 2 billion dollars in his wallet.
Or maybe it's because she lives in Atlanta now,
and in the South, they don't have much use
for logic, justice *or* good taste.

Every year, they celebrate the anniversary
of the civil rights March on Washington
led by Martin Luther King over 30 years ago.
What's to celebrate?
How marching doesn't work?

The government pays millions of dollars for studies
to answer questions like: "Does
racism play a role in the fact that black people
die at higher rates from heart attacks because
of inferior emergency medical care?"
They could save the money, and just ask me.
The answer is : "Yes."

Black Entertainment Television is
really taking a stand against
black-on-black crime.
It's banning videos that depict gunplay--
for a month.

Disparity in prison sentences for black and white
criminals is unfair.
But to the crybaby black criminals:
If you didn't deal the drugs, commit the robberies
and rapes, or do the murders
--usually harming *other* black people--
you wouldn't have to
worry about disparity in sentences,
now, would you?

Why do black people run that,
"It's just because he's black," mantra
whenever a black man, like
O.J. Simpson, Michael Jackson, or Mike Tyson
is accused of a crime.
You don't see Latinos saying,
"They're picking on them just because they're Latino,"
about the Menendez brothers or
Night Stalker Richard Ramirez.

O. J. Simpson: An instance when black
women can be glad that a successful
black man was obsessed with a white woman --
instead of one of them.

Many black men are like O.J. Simpson
and want white women.
And black women should encourage that.
Because for black women that would leave
white men, who, after all, are
the men with the *real* money.

Black men are always telling black women
to stay away from white men,
because, they say, all white men want
from black women is sex.
Of course, we've yet to hear
what that other thing is
that black men want from black women.

All women should avoid
any white guy who is poor or unsuccessful.
A man who can't make it
in a system where all the cards are
stacked in his favor,
surely ain't shit.

Hey guys, I'm just calling it
the way I see it,
and if the ballbuster fits...

Men think women must be stupid or something.
Like this one guy I met.
He was not that bright, and he was really mean to me.
He wasn't good-looking, and he was terrible in bed.
And this guy had the nerve to ask me to marry him!
And so...I did...

Men always make sure a woman knows when her
jeans are getting too tight.
So women are always trying to lose that
problem weight.
For a while, I was carrying a lot of extra weight, too.
But, then, luckily, I divorced him.

But my last husband was a *real* catch --
one I should've thrown back.

My latest ex-husband is a very stupid man.
When I left him, he had the nerve to say to me,
"You'll never be anything on your own.
You're just gonna go out and find some other
man you can live off of!"
What a dumb thing to say. Men are still
the ones with all the money, right?

Since I've been married so many times, I've
been asked if it's me who's the problem.
And when I think about it seriously,
I honestly have to say, "No, it was them."

I've been with rich men and I've been with poor men.
Rich is better.
I've been with tall men and I've been with short men.
Tall is better.
And men with hair versus balding men?
I completely avoid men who are losing their hair.
A woman has to draw the line somewhere.

Men can be pretty dumb.
Also insensitive, obnoxious, egotistical, violent,
self-centered, boring, chauvinistic...
And women can be pretty dumb, too --
for putting up with men.

Too bad sexual preference is determined at birth,
because if it wasn't,
there'd still be some hope for me.

If only I were a lesbian!
Then all my troubles --
notwithstanding Sandra Bernhard --
would be over.

My mother tried to tell me I'm too tough
on guys and that men really can
be good companions.
Well, I already have two very good friends --
my right hand... and my left.